Emmy
the Exaggerating
Elephant

Fenton
the Fearful Frog

Gertie
the Grungy Goat

He...
the Happy
Hamster

...
the Impatient
Iguana

Ollie
the Obedient
Ostrich

Perry
the Polite
Porcupine

Queenie
the Quiet Quail

Rupert
the Resourceful
Rhinoceros

Wendy
the Wise
Woodchuck

Xavier
the X-ploring
Xenops

Yori
the Yucky Yak

Ziggy
the Zippy Zebra

NOTE TO PARENTS

<u>Wendy's Clubhouse</u>
A story about wisdom

In this story, Wendy the Wise Woodchuck uses familiar proverbs and quotations to inspire her AlphaPet friends through the trials and tribulations they encounter as they build a clubhouse.

In addition to enjoying this charming story with your child, you can use it to teach a gentle lesson about good judgment and about the meaning of the golden rule: Treat others the way you would want to be treated yourself.

You can also use this story to introduce the letter **W**. As you read about Wendy the Wise Woodchuck, ask your child to listen for all the **W** words and point to the objects with names that begin with **W**. When you've finished reading the story, your child will enjoy doing the activity at the end of the book.

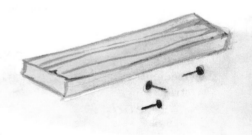

The AlphaPets™ characters were conceived and created by Ruth Lerner Perle.
Characters interpreted and designed by Deborah Colvin Borgo.
Cover/book design and production by Norton & Company.
Logo design by Deborah Colvin Borgo and Nancy S. Norton.
Grolier Books is a Division of Grolier Enterprises, Inc.   Printed and Manufactured in the United States of America

Wendy's Clubhouse

RUTH LERNER PERLE

Illustrated by Judy Blankenship

GROLIER
B O O K S

One Wednesday, the AlphaPets were at Wendy the Wise Woodchuck's house looking through books and newspapers. Nelly the Naughty Newt held up a page of the newspaper she was reading. "Hey, look at this!" she said, pointing to an advertisement. "Here's an ad for a Do-It-Yourself Clubhouse at Waldo's Wood Works."

"That's great!" shouted Ivy the Impatient Iguana. "Let's build a clubhouse!"

Wendy looked around her crowded living room. "We could use more room. Our Wednesday get-together group has been growing," she said. "A clubhouse is just what we need, and we can build it in the yard right near my favorite weeping willow tree."

"But building a house is a lot of work!" said Lizzy the Lazy Lamb.

"Lots of work," said Monty.

"And hammers and nails can be dangerous," added Fenton the Fearful Frog.

"Yes, dangerous," Monty said.

"Besides," said Una the Unhappy Unicorn. "We don't know how to build a house!"

Wendy pointed to a sign on her wall that read: *Nothing ventured, nothing gained.*

"If we don't try, we won't know if we can do it," she said.

"How are we going to pay for the clubhouse?" Nelly asked. "A do-it-yourself kit costs lots of money."

"Don't worry," Wendy said. "We'll each chip in as much money as we can."

So everybody took out their wallets. But when Emmy the Exaggerating Elephant looked into hers, it was empty.

"Oh, dear," Emmy said. "I don't have any money. Not a cent! I must have spent it all yesterday."

"*A penny saved is a penny earned*," said Wendy.

"You're right," said Emmy, nodding her head sadly. "If I had saved my money yesterday, I'd have some today."

Wendy counted the money. There was just enough for the building kit.

"There's no time to lose," she said. "As my great uncle used to say, '*The early bird catches the worm.*'"

"Well, then, we'd better get that kit right away so we can start building first thing tomorrow," Ollie the Obedient Ostrich added.

"Waldo's Wood Works is near your house, Lizzy," Wendy said. "Will you pick up the kit for us?"

THE EARLY
BIRD
CATCHES
THE
WORM

Lizzy looked up from her comfortable place on the sofa and rubbed her eyes.

"I guess I could pick up the kit," she said. "But I hope it's not too heavy for me to pull in my wagon."

"Your wagon has strong wheels," Emmy said. "You shouldn't have any trouble."

"Well, then," Ollie said, "you'd better get going! Waldo's will be closing soon."

"Yes, closing soon," added Monty.

So Lizzy waved good-bye and rushed off.

When Lizzy got home, she wheeled her wagon out of the garage and started pulling it across the lawn. Suddenly she felt very tired from all the rushing.

"Phew! This is hard work," she said. "Maybe I'll just rest for a moment before I go to Waldo's." Lizzy wiped her forehead and sat down under the wisteria tree. Before she knew it, she had leaned back, closed her eyes, and fallen fast asleep.

By the time Lizzy woke up, the
sun was setting. She looked at her
watch and said, "Oh, no! Look at
the time! Waldo's must be
closed now. I'll have to wait
until tomorrow to get
the building kit."

The next morning, right after breakfast, Lizzy went to Waldo's as fast as she could to buy the clubhouse kit.

When she entered the store she saw a big sign that read: SOLD OUT! MORE KITS COMING NEXT WEEK.

"Oh, no!" Lizzy thought to herself. "We wanted to start building our clubhouse today! Everyone is waiting at Wendy's house!"

So Lizzy ordered a kit and then she went to tell her friends the bad news.

DO-IT-YOURSELF CLUBHOUSE KITS

SOLD OUT!

MORE KITS COMING NEXT WEEK

SALE

All the AlphaPets were waiting at Wendy's house.

When Lizzy arrived, she told them what had happened.

"Well, that goes to show you, *never put off till tomorrow what you can do today*," Wendy said.

"What does that mean?" Lizzy asked.

"It means that if something has to be done, we should do it as soon as possible," Wendy explained.

"If you had gone right to Waldo's yesterday, we'd have our clubhouse today," Nelly said.

"I meant to, but . . ." Lizzy said.

"Never mind," Ollie said, smiling. "A week is not too long to wait. We can think about how we want to decorate our clubhouse."

On the day the kit was to arrive, Ivy and Albert the Absent-minded Alligator volunteered to wait for it. The others went to buy some food for lunch.

When the do-it-yourself clubhouse kit arrived, Ivy was all excited. "Let's get started!" she shouted.

"Yes, yes, let's get started!" Albert agreed.

They opened the box and took out all the pieces.

"How do we put it together?" Albert asked. "Where are the instructions?"

"There's no time to look for instructions," Ivy said. "Let's hurry so we can surprise everybody when they come back." She took her hammer and some nails and started to work.

"Well, OK," Albert said, and he started to hammer, too.

When the AlphaPets returned with the
food, they couldn't believe their eyes.

"Oh, no!" cried Lizzy.

"That's the silliest thing I've ever seen!" Nelly shouted.

"The door is on the roof," Emmy giggled.

"The window is where the door belongs," Ollie groaned.

"The roof sticks out at the side!" Fenton muttered.

"Just as my grandma always says, '*Haste makes
waste*,'" said Wendy. "We should take time to plan
ahead and do things right."

"Now we can't have a clubhouse," Una cried. "It's all ruined!"

"Yes, ruined," added Monty.

"Don't worry," said Wendy. "*If at first you don't succeed, try and try again.*"

So everybody rolled up their sleeves and got to work, taking the pieces apart.

Ollie found the instructions inside the packing carton and slowly but surely, the AlphaPets put the clubhouse together the right way.

When the AlphaPets were finished building their clubhouse, they stepped back to admire it.

"Now, all we have to do is paint it," Ollie said, reading the instructions.

Everybody dipped their brushes in paint. They painted the inside light blue, the outside bright yellow, and the door brick-red. In no time at all, the whole house was painted.

The instructions said to wait one hour for the paint to dry before adding the finishing touches.

So everyone had lunch and a drink of water from the well. Everyone, that is, except Ivy.

She was too excited to wait for the paint to dry. Ivy ran to the clubhouse and pushed the door open so she could peek inside.

Squish! her hand smeared the wet paint, and her fingerprints made messy marks all over the sticky door.

"Yikes!" Ivy cried, looking at the mess she made. "The paint is still wet!"

The AlphaPets saw what happened and came running.

"Oh, Ivy!" Una cried. "Our clubhouse is ruined!"

"I'm sorry. I didn't mean . . . . I was only trying . . ." mumbled Ivy.

"Don't worry. We have enough extra paint to smooth out the smudges," Wendy said. "But next time Ivy, try to remember: *Look before you leap!*"

Everybody helped Ivy touch up the smudges and then they waited patiently for the paint to dry.

While the AlphaPets were admiring their good work, Ollie took his paints and went inside. After a few minutes he came out again with a sign under his arm. Then he gathered everyone around and said, "If it weren't for Wendy's wonderful words of wisdom to encourage us, we wouldn't have a clubhouse at all."

Ollie held up the sign he had painted. It read: WENDY'S CLUBHOUSE. Then he hung it on the clubhouse door.

Just then, Perry the Polite Porcupine, Katy the Kind Koala, Xavier the X-ploring Xenops, and Connie the Cuddly Cat came by.

"Oooh! What a beautiful clubhouse," Katy said.

"May we come in?" asked Perry the Polite Porcupine.

"No!" shouted Nelly. "Only those who helped build this house can be in the club. You can't join."

Perry, Katy, Xavier, and Connie felt sad. They turned around and started to leave, but Wendy ran after them.

WENDY'S CLUBHOUSE

EVERYBODY WELCOME

"No, no, no," said Wendy smiling warmly. "Come back, dear friends."

Then she turned to Nelly. "Of all words of wisdom," Wendy added, "the most important are *do unto others as you would have them do unto you.* We should always treat people the way we would want to be treated. Don't you think it will be more fun to share our clubhouse?"

"I guess so," said Nelly, slightly embarrassed for being so rude. "I'm sorry," she added as she took Katy's hand and led her toward the clubhouse door.

Then Wendy picked up Ollie's paintbrush and painted another sign.

The AlphaPets watched as Wendy hung the new sign under the other one.

It read: EVERYBODY WELCOME.

All the AlphaPets clapped and cheered, agreeing that that was the best advice of all.

Be wise. Please learn these wonderful words with me.

wallet

worm

wagon

window

watch

wheel

well

Look back at the pictures in this book and try to find these and other things that begin with the letter W.

Aa Bb

Gg Hh

Mm Nn Oo Pp

Uu Vv Ww